DOOBY

Other Novels by Bruce Brooks

Asylum for Nightface

What Hearts

Everywhere

No Kidding

Midnight Hour Encores

The Moves Make the Man

THE WOLFBAY WINGS

Woodsie

Zip

Cody

Boot

Prince

Shark

Billy

Reed

BRUCE BROOKS

A LAURA GERINGER BOOK
An Imprint of HarperCollins*Publishers*

Library of Congress Cataloging-in-Publication Data
Brooks, Bruce.
    Dooby / Bruce Brooks.
        p.   cm. — (Wolfbay Wings ; #8)
    "A Laura Geringer book."
    Summary: Fully expecting to be elected captain of his ice hockey team, Dooby is dismayed when the position goes to the new player because she is a girl.
    ISBN 0-06-440708-X (pbk.) — ISBN 0-06-027898-6 (lib. bdg.)
    [1. Hockey—Fiction.   2. Sex role—Fiction.]   I. Title.
II. Series: Brooks, Bruce.   Wolfbay Wings ; #8.
PZ7.B7913Do   1998   98-24715
[Fic]—dc21   CIP
                                                                    AC

Typography by Steve Scott
1   2   3   4   5   6   7   8   9   10
❖
First Edition

Visit us on the World Wide Web!
http://www.harperchildrens.com

As I walked into the locker room on the first day of hockey practice, my very first day as a Peewee, which is the stupid name for the next level up from the even more stupidly designated Squirts, I could not help noticing something that had nothing to do with hockey. You know how it is—when you're curious, you can't help picking up signals from anything that seems to be sending them.

Well, that first day, when my antennae were fully extended and I was taking readings on whatever I could, I noticed—first thing, without trying— that some of these very mature fellows who so proudly called themselves Peewees seemed to believe they needed to *shave.* Because there, standing over a sink in front of a mirror, contorting a face covered with white foam and preparing to scrape it with a razor I could only assume was loaded with a genuine lethally sharp metal blade, was a second year Peewee named Sandy Beckstein, who was, at the very most, barely twelve years old and whose skin was almost certainly as hairless as mine.

Is *that* what makes you a true Peewee?

—What're you doing? I asked Sandy at just the moment he started an upstroke along his neck. He jumped a little, as I had hoped, and, sure enough, some blood started to discolor his foam.

His eyes looked for mine in the mirror and found them. I'm practicing my backhand, Dork-breath, he said. Then he lifted his razor, which looked like a raygun from an old space movie, and actually did swipe it across his cheek back-handed.

—Nice, I said. Now let's see you stickhandle.

But before Sandy could figure out how to re-spond to that, Pincher Greene, another of last year's Peewees, spoke up very loudly from a bench.

—Quiet! Here comes—just another hockey player!

The door opened and a girl dressed in a Wings practice sweater and the rest of the hockey equip-ment walked in.

I looked at her, then over at Cody, generally a

modest guy, who had everything off but his cup pants, and Zip, far from modest, who had everything off but his jock.

Zip smiled warmly at the girl and with one thumb held the waistband of his jock three inches out from his stomach.

—Quarter for a peek, he said.

The girl, who had not returned his smile, dumped her bag on the floor, took a bored look at Zip, and sat down on the bench.

—Nope, she said. You'd have to pay me at least a buck to look in there.

—I meant—

—She knows what you meant, puckhead, said Cody. She made a funny.

—Oh, said Zip. I get it. Instead of her paying— oh, ho ho.

—I thought it was pretty good, Cody said.

—Then you get to center her line, said Pincher.

—I probably will, said Cody. Is she any good?

—*That* will cost more than a quarter to find out, said Pincher.

—I meant—

But the girl waved Cody quiet and said, I know

what you meant, and the answer, *free*, is that I am not very good *but* I would appreciate you letting this guy keep building up his large inventory of primitive innuendos, because the Supreme Court will be putting him away for a long time any day now. She looked at the rest of us. See, it is illegal for you to notice that I am gender-differentiated from you he-men. In fact, as the boys here will help me tell you on three, I am—one, two, and-uh-three—

—*Just another hockey player*, hollered Sandy and Pincher and the girl.

—So, Peewee teammates! I said, rubbing my hands. We Peewees shave, and we share our locker room with gender-undifferentiated girls—but is there any *real* difference from Squirts?

—Yeah, said Sandy. By now he had scraped most of his foam off. Yeah: Up here we don't lose twenty-nine games.

—We'll just see about *that*, I said with a chuckle. There's a fresh new wind blowin' into this team, and it's capable of sweeping—

—Do you always talk this much? the girl asked me.

—Always, said Woodsie as he walked through the door.

—So you *didn't* take that scholarship to the quantum mechanics lab at MIT after all! I said to him.

—Who are you? Pincher asked him.

—He's the Duke of Earl, said Cody.

—The Sultan of Swat, said Zip.

—The Pause That Refreshes, said Woodsie.

—His name is Woods and he is going to take your job, Beckstein said as he felt up and down his throat.

Pincher is a defenseman who skates very pretty and thus always makes travel teams. But he has one bad habit, and it is enough to make him almost useless. When a defenseman chooses not to hold his point position or to backskate once the other guys have taken possession of the puck, but instead chases the puck *into* his offensive zone, he is said to be "pinching." Pinching usually results in the other guys' skating by the defenseman in a whoosh and getting a two-on-one the other way. As you might gather from his name, Pincher finds it impossible not to leave his post and chase after the puck whenever it comes within fifteen feet of him. He rarely gets it. Goalies, who tend to fare poorly against two-on-ones, despise him, as do many coaches. But he does skate so pretty. . . .

—Are you really a defenseman? he asked Woodsie, and Woodsie nodded. Pincher groaned and uttered a very bad word.

—What did you expect, Pinch? I said. Did you think the Squirts didn't have any defensemen or something?

—Well, he said through his sulk, you *did* lose a million games.

—It was the goaltending and the goaltending alone, said Cody.

—Here's another one, Beckstein said as Barry shuffled in. And *he's* better than you are too, Pinch, *way* better.

—Are you? Pinch asked.

—Am I what? Barry said cautiously.

—A better defenseman than I am.

—Oh, said Barry, unslinging his bag and letting it fall. Oh, def.

Pinch said another bad word and added, How many D are you guys bringing up, anyway?

—Jeez, why don't you whine or something? said the girl.

—Why don't *you* grow a goatee? Pinch snapped.

—Now, boys! I said. And of course, ladies—

—First of all, there isn't but one of me, so keep it singular, and second, remember that the Supreme Court is all set to jump all over your tail and ruin the rest of your life: phone taps, twenty-four-hour surveillance, saltpeter in your food . . .

—Sorry, I said. But what *do* I call you?

—Hey, said Barry, noticing her for the first time and gaping.

—Careful, she said to him. Under certain statutes, staring may be interpreted as a form of sexual harassment. To me she said, You may call me Nathan.

—Nathan.

—For half the season last year her daddums had to come in here and hand her each piece of equipment to make sure she got it on just right, Pincher said in an ugly voice.

—My father is a dip, she said with a sigh. He is unconvinced that I can breathe unless he is here to contribute the influence of his male knowledge of the universe's mechanics.

—How did you get rid of him? I asked.

The boys came up with the very sophisticated technique of engaging in an endless relay of mouth-farts, she said. It finally drove him away.

—You should have heard us, Pincher laughed. We were awesome. He issued a fairly decent mouth-fart to demonstrate, but no one, not even Beckstein, followed up.

—Why Nathan? I asked her.

She shrugged. It's about as far as you can get from Kathy, she said, which is my gender-differentiated name.

—Did the others call you Nathan in front of your father? Woodsie asked.

—Oh, certainly, she said. He thought they were referring to someone else, a player he never managed to identify all year, even though he kept statistics on the entire team.

—Oh, no, said Zip. Not one of *those* fathers.

—I'm afraid so, she said. But don't worry. He only kept plus–minus, and as a goalie you are ineligible for the Widgeon Award.

—The what? about five of us asked.

—It's his own award, Beckstein said, which he presents in a personal ceremony to the player who leads his daughter's team in that particular, much-underrated statistic. He buys a little trophy and everything.

—Who won last year? I asked.

—Sandy did, said Pincher. And don't let him pretend he didn't keep the trophy. It's probably the only one he'll ever get and he knows it.

—As a matter of fact, Beckstein said, and much to your shame for not noticing, Pincher, I snuck in here two nights after the season ended and arc-welded the figurine onto the Zamboni as a kind of hood ornament.

—No way! said Pincher.

—It's true that there is a trophy figurine on the Zamboni, Woodsie said. One that was not there last year.

Beckstein smiled smugly, and said, Whoever wins this season will have to think of something different.

—If I call you Nathan, said Zip, will you call me Maria?

—Sure, Nathan said. Kiss my cup, Maria.

—Which one? Zip said. You have two.

—Three, she said.

—What's the third one for? Cody asked sincerely.

—That will cost you a quarter to find out, said Nathan. Plus a trip to the Supreme Court and a few calendars in the federal slammer.

In little bunches the rest of the guys drifted in—Ernie and Java and Prince and the Boot, who actually blushed when he looked at Nathan and, as far as I could tell, never looked at her again for the duration of the season. Most of last year's Squirts moved up to the Peewee A team, just as most of last year's Peewees went to Bantams. Only Pincher and Sandy and the girl are left from last year's Peewee team, which went about .500.

—Hey, goalie, said Sandy. Is your hundred-goal pal Moseby a Peewee this year, or did he stay a Squirt?

—Oh, he's a Peewee, said Zip. His birthday's two weeks before mine.

Sandy cussed bitterly and said, Well, there go the Montrose games. Then, as if on cue, Kenny Moseby himself walked into the room with his bag on his shoulder, nodding a shy hello to everyone.

Sandy gaped. Is he— Are you playing for *us*? he said.

—Why else would he be here, Foamface? Zip said.

Sandy hooted and threw both fists in the air. Kenny tried to ignore him by digging into his bag, but I saw his neck blush.

—Looks like you can kiss those hopes of repeating as the Widgeon winner good-bye, said Woodsie. Then he walked over and quietly introduced himself to Kenny with a handshake and a few murmured words. It was a formality—they'd played against each other several times last year—but it's just the sort of gentlemanly touch Woodsie would see was needed to break the wowie-zowie bit Beckstein started. It worked; nobody else reacted to Kenny's presence except by saying hello, or Welcome back. His neck went back to its normal color.

—Politeness, said Cody, shaking his head. Sensitivity. Jeez, it's going to be a funny year.

—Oh, goody! Zip squealed. I just *adore* humor! Does anyone know any off-color limericks?

—There once was a team from Wolf*bay*—I started.

—Stop it right *now*, said Zip, or I will honest to goodness wet my *pants*.

—You people are peculiar, said Nathan.

The Boot just shook his head and got dressed. Moseby pulled on his skates. Woodsie, all dressed, leaned silently against the wall. Barry looked around in general disgust. The door swung open and for a second no one was there. Then Shinny hopped in on crutches with one leg in a long cast.

—Oh, great! said Barry with even more disgust, throwing a sock into his bag. What happened to you?

—Bessaball been berry berry good to me, said Shinny, as he dropped to a bench and propped his busted leg on his crossed crutches.

—You broke your leg playing *baseball*? Zip asked incredulously.

—Yep.

—What happened? asked Cody. Like, a high-speed, blindside collision in the outfield or something?

—Something like that, Shinny said.

—Nonsense, said Woodsie. We all looked at him. I was at the game because my sister plays on the other team. Shinny took a huge cut at a change-up, missed it by a foot, and somehow managed to smash himself in the leg with his aluminum bat. And I mean smash it *fat*, said Woodsie. He got it *all*.

Shinny shrugged.

Kenny was staring at Shinny in utter disbelief. To Kenny there is no sport—in fact, no reason for breathing—other than ice hockey. Shinny gave him a wave and said, Hey, K. Still good for three hundred points?

Moseby blushed and dropped his eyes.

—Who's coaching? Shinny asked. I heard they canned your old man, Codes.

—Yeah, said Cody, pulling his sweater over his head. He wasn't macho enough with us last year. Didn't show that hunger to win that we all like to see on a Wolfbay team.

—Right, I said. That special hunger and brilliant strategies that just *might* have turned some of those twelve-goal losses into ten-goal losses.

—Did they really blame your *dad*? Shinny said. We reeked, all by ourselves.

—And it was only thanks to him we got better at the end, said Barry.

—No, no, said Zip. That was the goaltending.

Ignoring him, Prince said, Even my grandfather was impressed with Coach Cooper.

There was a moment of awed silence while the profound import of this sank in for the new Peewees. We all know Prince's grandfather well, and know that almost *nothing* impresses him, though he notices absolutely everything that happens on the ice in every practice and game and is not at all shy about giving you a very precise lecture about how you should have never been holding your stick blade against the ice at a certain angle even though the puck was in the corner ninety feet away, because if the puck happened to strike your stick blade just *so* . . . Nobody minds these lectures, largely because we all really like Prince's grandfather and appreciate his attention but also because usually by the third sentence he has gotten so excited he has forgotten to speak English and the rest comes in his cool-sounding French, at approximately eight words a second.

—Your grandfather comes to the games? asked Nathan. I imagine she was thinking Prince, being a black hockey player and therefore a bizarre aberration in his family, was probably scorned by all his bloods, who must play basketball instead. Common mistake.

—His grandfather comes to *showers*, said Cody.

—We don't have showers in our locker rooms, Cody.

—But if we did, said Prince, it is true that my grandpop would probably be unable in certain crucial cases to restrain himself from following whoever he was talking to about the misplaced center of gravity of a second-period hipcheck right under the spray.

—In his suit, of course, said Zip.

—*Not* taking time to remove the silk pocket handkerchief, said Woodsie.

I looked at Nathan. His grandfather was born in Montreal, so hockey is kind of important to him, I told her.

—That's a city in France, Zip added helpfully. So he mostly speaks French.

—They *love* hockey over there across the great Atlantic, said Cody.

—Yeah, said Prince. When I think of the number

of great French players who have filled NHL rosters since—

The door opened and again there was a delay before the person opening it showed himself. This time, jumping quickly through and into the room and flattening himself along the wall, looking over his shoulder at the door and panting, it was Cody's dad, wearing his warm-ups and skates but also one of those ten-cent fake nose-mustache-glasses things.

—Help! said Zip, putting a hand to his forehead. I suddenly feel I am about to fall in love with losing for losing's sake!

—De*feat* is *sweet*, Woodsie chanted, joined by four or five others.

Coach Cooper pulled off the disguise. Hello, Peewees, he said. And thanks for the welcome. You guys would mock a double amputee.

—First we'd challenge him to a footrace, Zip said.

—What if the 'double' referred to his arms, and he still had both legs? Prince asked.

—Then, after he beat me in the footrace, I would pound the crap out of him with both of *my* hands.

—Are you our coach? asked Kenny, sounding hopeful.

—I have that honor, Coach Coop said with a bow. All the old Squirts cheered. He held up his hands to stop us.

—But I must warn you, he said, that I am not the same old softy you so craftily enjoy taking advantage of. No. It is true that the fellow who was going to coach you came down with mononucleosis, and that there was absolutely no one else the board could think of who would bear the insult of being asked to step in so late, *but*— he shakes a finger at us—I have been given this opportunity only if I promise to become a nastier, shiftier, more cutthroat kind of guy. So be warned: This season, I am pulling out every trick in the bag—we are going hell-bent for that elusive nineteen-loss figure, no matter what the cost to your self-esteem.

We all cheered. You're *just* the guy who can lose only nineteen, said Shinny. We all have faith in you.

—Even these ringers from last year's team, said Zip, looking at the three of them, who mostly didn't know what to think or do. Isn't that *right?* he yelled.

—Certainly, said Sandy. I would definitely get behind a team goal of losing less than twenty-nine.

—Count me in, said Nathan. I'm *much* more of a nineteen-loss kind of player.

Pincher was out of his league, though. Frowning, trying hard to get it, he said, Do we, like, *have* to lose nineteen?

—It's a point of honor, said Woodsie. Didn't you hear the man?

—Could we maybe lose even fewer? Pincher asked meekly.

We all started lecturing him in nonsense at once, until Coach tooted his whistle. We all shut up and looked at him.

—I want you on the ice in sixty seconds, he said, and then left.

A couple of guys cussed and hustled to tie their skates and snap their helmets, whatever the last steps were, and everyone else crowded the door. Pincher was still sitting, perplexed.

—This guy jokes with you like that, he coaches you to the worst season anybody ever had in this club—but when he says jump, you still jump?

—He's the Coach, Pinch, I said.

Pinch shook his head, but then he jammed his helmet on in a hurry and made it onto the ice in time.

two

We weren't too bad for the first skate, really. We were all different in this practice than we were in tryouts; everybody knew this was our first real look at each other. Because almost the whole team was together last year, there weren't any big surprises. Still, a couple of things stood out.

One was that Nathan can really fly. In fact, she's not only extremely fast, she can maneuver really well in tight spaces, what's called "making ice for herself," and backwards she may be almost as fast as Cody. I am impressed. But I would be even more impressed if she kept her stick blade on the ice or held her stick with both hands all the time or showed some of that sudden sprint-speed when a puck got past her into a corner. Nathan showed no inclination to get in there and fight for it when it's all elbows and butts and knees. I tried not to be sexist about this.

The second surprise, as always, was just how incredible Kenny Moseby is. Not just how *good* he is, which is amazing enough; but how inspired and fresh and excited he is, acting as if every drill is going to be his final chance to experience the joys of ice-skating in his life. It's not "acting" as in "faking." This is how K lives, once he has skates on: Nothing is done except at full speed, with reckless abandon. He hurls himself after every loose puck, he spins tight as a geometry lesson around every cone, he skates all the way to each line in line drills—while everyone else kind of cheats and stops a little short and a little soft and coasts to within a foot or two, Kenny skates to the line and stops dead on it from full tilt to zero in one big spray, but before the crystals have fallen he has taken off back to the next line. If we had anyone but Coach Coop, who has known K since he was about four, we'd probably all think Moze was kissing up and making us all look bad. But Coach knows better than to expect the rest of us humans to match Kenny. He also knows that being around Kenny *does* tend to make anyone go a *little* harder than he otherwise might, out of a feeling that arises somewhere between competitiveness and inspiration.

Everything else was as usual. Zip was moaning and sitting down and stuff, acting like he generally had a harder job than anybody and got paid way less. Plus he was panting from skating half the length of the ice at half-speed on his way to the cage.

—Zip, said the coach at one point. Do you know what your best single feature is?

—That would be the unique color of my eyes, Zip said, which is a very rare shade of blue often called 'cobalt'—

—Your best feature, at least the only one I can figure keeps landing you on travel teams, is being the son of the rink manager, said Coach. How in the world—I mean, it was *nice* out this summer—how did you manage to avoid getting into any kind of playing condition?

—Practice, Coach, said Zip. A careful regimen of practice, practice, practice. You'd be surprised what an inert slug you can become if you work hard enough at it.

I noticed Prince had grown some over the summer and gotten stronger—the first couple of times I tried to pry him off the puck in a corner using the same leverage and effort that had worked last year, he just shrugged me off. That was good.

I noticed Cody, already the smallest player on the team, seemed to have maybe shrunk by a couple of inches. That was not good. But then, Codes is such a supreme skater that there is almost no one who can get enough of a hold on him to apply any muscle.

Woodsie and Billy had obviously been to camp (as had Zip and I, but we goofed around a lot). Woodsie had just as obviously spent a good few hours thinking about the game, whereas Billy had clearly *not* thought about it one second once camp was over. Billy's dad is always talking hockey to him, and I believe Billy lets that take the place of doing any thinking on his own.

In our first okay-let's-really-try scrimmage, the Blacks beat the Blues 8–2. Kenny, who did not seem to dominate the game in any particular way, scored seven of those goals. Seven. Looking back as carefully as you like, you could not say you have the memory of him carrying the puck more than anybody else, nor could you recall grand rushes in which he wound his way resolutely through the entire defense, driven by pure will to the inevitable score. You just remember he was always in the right spot, playing his position; he always had his head up and his stick down; he always played hard. And somehow it added up to the astonishing number of seven goals.

Maybe it's because I'm a defenseman, but probably not—in any case, if I look back and remember any particular play of Kenny's during a game or scrimmage, it's almost always a defensive play. He always shuts down his own man, but keeps one eye on the rest of the ice and the guys and the puck and where everything is and how fast it's moving in which direction, so when danger is about to strike because somebody gets turned around or misjudges an angle for a check, well, then suddenly Kenny is on the spot to backcheck a two-on-one into a harmless two-on-two, or to poke-check a rushing winger with one awkwardly turned man to beat at the blue line for a breakaway.

Those are my favorite K-plays, and *they* don't even show up in his stats. They show up on the scoreboard, though, as "non goals," and in close games they can be decisive.

I make a point of mentioning several of these plays to Kenny whenever I'm on the ice with him, because I suspect he likes the semi-secrecy of them better than the gaudy goals–assists totals he always rings up, which anyone can see and gawk over. He always thanks me and mumbles something about getting lucky, but we both know better.

I like to think that if I were the best player in the area, maybe one of the best fifty in the country, I would be all shy and blushy like Kenny. But I probably wouldn't. Probably, I'd strut and trumpet, never letting my lips go cold, as Zip puts it when he marvels at my active mouth.

Actually, there are times when my mouth is useful in a hockey game: I chatter at opponents and if one of them is a hothead who can be distracted by words, I will get him off his game; I talk to my teammates, and with them I don't just mess—it is important to communicate on coverage, pass options, all kinds of things; and lastly, I sometimes talk to the referee and linesmen. Not to whine, and not to ask for obvious favors and stuff like that, but to mention a foul an opponent is getting away with behind their backs, or to calmly disagree with an offside call, or to represent the team's interests when something complicated is being called.

Secretly—one would never be vocal about *this*—I hope my mouth will get me elected captain of the team this year.

Electing the captain is one of those mysterious processes that seems to just get taken care of behind the scenes by the leaders of the team; when the actual voting takes place, everyone already knows who has been chosen, and it's merely a formality to elect him. Before this season, as one of the team leaders, I have always been in on the consulting, along with Prince and Cody and Barry and maybe Shinny. We kick around a name in a pretend-casual way, veto it or support it, let it simmer for a few days, then pass the word.

There is a new captain every season, and of course he has to act as if it is no big deal. But I suppose I was hoping finally to kind of cash in on the big mouth. Make it work for something besides a few laughs. It meant a lot to me, and I think my buddies knew it, because during a break in the scrimmage, while I was leaning against the boards, Prince skated over and hung an elbow beside mine.

—What do you think? he said, lifting his chin at the people skating. It was purely a way of starting some real talk.

—Okay, I said. You're looking pretty strong, and Beckstein seems to like the grind stuff, which is good, and the girl can move. And of course there's Kenny.

Prince nodded. Cody skated up and sat on his stick between us. Girl's fast, he said. But she's got the heart of a sparrow.

—Can't teach 'em to want it, said Prince, and we all laughed, because that used to be the favorite cliché of one of our Mite coaches. He usually hollered it so the parents could hear just after we had given up a goal or missed a good chance to score one.

—We're thinking, said Prince, still watching the players skating around.

—Yeah? I said, my heart picking up a few beats.

—Yeah, said Cody. This captain thing. You interested?

—We like the idea of you yapping for us, Prince said, giving me a "decorous interval," as they used to call it in ballroom dancing class, to pretend to consider the idea. You're on the ice more than anyone, too—and your playing is really getting great.

—Thanks, I said. And, yeah, I guess I'm interested. I'd like it okay.

—'Nuff said. Prince still hadn't even looked at me. He nodded and pushed off the boards, and swiped the puck from Woodsie and took it in on Zip and shot high, which Zip hates, especially early in the year. He ducked and the shot went in.

—*Got* some guts, hollered Nathan.

—Got some other things even better than guts, Zip said.

—Keep them to yourself like a nice boy.

—You're not allowed to notice I'm a boy.

—You're right. As a matter of fact, as far as I'm concerned, technically the question is still up in the air.

—Okay, said Coach, blowing his whistle. Let's skate some lines.

—What's this 'we' stuff? said Zip. You last skated lines in the 1940s.

—Okay, Zip, said Coach, just one time, for you, and he lined up to skate them with us.

Cody straightened up. If you want it, we want you, he said to me. We'll get word around by the election.

—Cool, I said. And that was that. I was ecstatic. I even skated right with Kenny for the first three lines. Then he left me in his ice dust.

It was kind of traditional that Cody had been the last to let me know, because he was the captain last year. And although he is *the* most naturally cool kid on the team and the most completely even-tempered, he just didn't have any fire to him. Frequently we had to tell him when a bogus penalty had been called and let him know he ought to say something, to which he always responded the same way: He skated by the ref and said, Hey, how you doing? and the ref would say, Fine, Cody, and that would be it.

Prince would make a great captain if it weren't for the very loud presence of his grandfather, who spouts passionately for the whole game, directing at least a third of his yelling at the refs, who do not like being yelled at in French. Because he is usually the only black fan, and Prince is the only black player, the link is obvious—and Prince couldn't help suffering a little get-back from the refs for his grandfather's outbursts.

Kenny Moseby is the team's best player, but that doesn't count for much. In fact, Prince once said the only sure way of getting K to sit a season would be to give him the C. He would bury himself in ice chips before ever saying a single word to an official, and he talks absolutely no trash with opponents either. Doesn't need to.

There is one purpose my mouth serves that I think the other players don't know about, even now. It's kind of cool, and the fact it's secret makes it even better: Coach Cooper calls me up on the phone a few times a week, just to talk about the team and stuff. He's a talker too, like me, and he just has to chatter. I really don't think even Cody knows.

Nobody but me talks so much in my family. They all do something else instead to express themselves, I guess. My mom paints, like oil paintings of fruit and stuff like that, things you put frames around. The paintings never look like fruit or whatever things they are supposed to show, but, according to her, the "discrepancy between visions" is for me to figure out.

My dad plays the piano, but not the easygoing sit-down-casually-and-flutter-the-hands-over-the-keys type of playing. No, sir, my dad plays with *rigor*: He belongs to an association of incredibly strict pianists who play nothing but certain kinds of pure ragtime written in certain years by certain composers in a certain rigidly defined style. If you ever meet one of these guys, let me give you a hint: Avoid as if they were viruses words such as *improvisation, interpretation, embellishment, experimentation.* What's weird with my dad's ragtime is, the music can sound very spontaneous and joyful and dreamy—as if the guy who wrote it thought it up in a quick twenty minutes of fooling around. It gives your feet a twitch sometimes when it's trottin' along; but to watch my dad sweating over a piece, and listening to him repeat a phrase hundreds of times, without any apparent variation, makes me want to ask where the fun went.

Neither Mom nor Dad talks much, but the quietest person in the family is my brother Moose. Moose can be counted on to speak to me on my birthday, when he says, Happy birthday, bro, and it sometimes seems that's all there is for the year. But like me, Moose plays hockey. Or, rather, not like me—because Moose is awesome, about half as good at his older age level as Kenny Moseby, which is saying something. Moose is awkward in every way off the ice—he gets straight C's in school, blows every attempt to talk to girls, has a best friend who just sits with him in his bedroom throwing a tennis ball back and forth, without a word. But on the ice Moose's eyes flash with alertness and—there's no other word for it—some creativity that is almost supernatural takes over and he does amazing things. He is a natural goal scorer, but where Kenny is kind of invisible, Moose is flashy. You can't take your eyes off him when he's on the ice, even if you never saw him play before—you just *know* this guy is going to make something happen, and chances are that on any given shift he *will*, he'll do something that brings you to your feet and makes you holler.

—Dad, I once asked, do you think I talk all the time because playing defense in ice hockey does not allow me to express myself fully?

He was bent over a score that seemed, to me, to have more notes on it than any single piece of paper ought to have.

—Yes, he said. I think you're probably right.

—Well, I said, taking a deep breath, then how come devoting yourself completely to the ideas of another person without deviating in the slightest from his notations allows you to express *yourself* so fully?

—Easy, he said, turning the page without looking up, and studying a whole new layout of sixty-fourth notes. Doing that allows me to express myself because I am, basically, a completely uninventive person who depends on others to show me exactly what to do.

He looked up and smiled. It's the truth, he said. Don't worry about bringing it up—I'm neither ashamed nor angry.

—Okay, I said. And Mom? Those weird paintings?

—She's the opposite. All invention, no direction. But that's just exactly who she is.

—And Moose?

My father just shook his head and sighed. I knew very well that he didn't think my brother's name belonged in the same paragraph with words such as *express* or *self* or *invention*. To him, Moose was a lower form of primate living entirely by instinct. I think this is only because Moose cannot talk about "expressing himself" but just goes out and *does* it.

—Your brother, he said, your brother is—well, he's just an athlete. No more, no less.

He made it sound as if that "no less" was a mere formality.

—And me? I said. Aren't I just an athlete too?

—No. You, to bring us full circle, are a hopeless chatterbox. I'd say hockey does very little for you in the self-expression mode. Maybe it just gives you something to talk about, since you have to be talking anyway. Who knows?

—*That*'s a relief, I said. It's hard enough playing it just as a plain old game without having to worry about it Meaning Big Things.

He looked up at me again and smiled.

—Meaning never comes through the door you are watching, he said. Still, I'd say you're pretty safe that it's not going to sneak up on you during a hockey game.

—What about Moose?

—Moose, he said, shaking his head. You would

have thought my brother's endless displays of pure talent were nothing more than a monkey chancing onto a way to get at the soft part of a banana.

—Why don't you respect his ability more? I asked.

—Because it's—it's nothing but pure physical instinct.

—So? We all got bodies, right? I mean, what do you play your rags with—your fingers, or what?

But he was looking up now and backward, at some important memory. I let him get it straight, and waited.

—See, I tried once, he said. I asked him, I asked your brother, at least a dozen times during one season. Just after a game was over I would go over in precise detail an incredible, ornate play he had pulled off, usually with no small amount of flourish. Dramatic, creative plays, things that involved such fascinating complexity. . . .

He sighed. But do you know what he said? Every single time?

—Yes. He said he didn't really remember making the play, certainly not thinking it out.

My father nodded. Exactly. He would just shrug

and say something like Sounds cool, or, If you say so, Dad, but I was just out there playin', not thinkin.

—But that's *it*, I said. That's *hockey*, the speed, it makes you do things you couldn't have dreamed up—

—Well, 'dreaming it up' and 'thinking' are what it's all about, he said. Not just dropping onto the ice and jumping into this blind, speedy action you seem to celebrate.

—Frankly, I don't like your music, either.

—It's a free country, he said with a wave.

—Not on your piano, I said, and ran off before he could think of a better closer.

The fact is, I was excited after that first scrimmage, because I could tell that even that one year had made a difference, moving up to Peewees was a real change, and it was a change in speed. Why it should be so, I don't know; but I knew this was going to be a season that demanded quicker decisions, snappier touches of the puck, faster reactions. I'm no Moose, but I can play, and I was looking forward to it.

The night after the scrimmage my mother called me to the phone.

—Hello? I said.

—I'm not what you'd call a devil, am I, Doobs? An evil man? A guy who deserves hell on earth?

It was Coach Cooper. No, Coach, I said. You know we all think you're the best guy in the world.

—Then why does the best guy in the world keep getting stuck with the crazies? I mean, I love the guy and all, but it took me three years before I felt I could breathe freely around Prince's grandfather. And Billy's dad—

—Who is it now? I asked, with a twiggle of misgiving in my stomach. Or what is it?

—That's a very wise way of asking, he said. Because it's not really a 'who,' although it's being passed off that way; it's really a 'what.'

My stomach dropped a foot. The girl, I said. You're being forced to do something to highlight the girl.

—I am. He sighed. And it's not even her fault— she didn't ask for any favors. It's her bleeping father and the bleeping board, which let the father tell them what a wonderful thing it would be for

Wolfbay to show how 'enlightened' it is with regard to the 'full breadth' of this great game's tremendous appeal, which reaches out to everyone regardless of age, color, gender, religion—

—You've been told to make her captain, I said.

He sighed again, and waited a respectful moment, and I wasn't sure whether Cody had told him or he'd just figured it out that I was going to be the one; Coach is sharp enough to notice these things all by himself. Anyway, after his respectful silence, he said, Yeah. That's what I have to do. I have to trample into places a coach has no right to go and blow off the one single decision that is and ought to be left to the players themselves, and I have to force the team's choice of its leader back into the pack and put this poor girl whose fate is now sealed—I mean, who won't hate her now?—onto a false pedestal, just so a couple of people can say, Hey, check it out. We got a girl *captain*, maybe we'll make *People* magazine like that Texas high school football team that put a girl soccer star on the field to kick extra points. You recall her name, Doobs?

—Slips my mind right now.

—How about the school? Or even the town?

I didn't think so. But that's the fame we are now chasing. But listen. Seriously.

—Okay.

—I will gladly refuse to do it. It will mean you'll get another coach, someone who *will* do it, so nothing will change except me. But I almost *want* to refuse—

—Please don't, I said. Just do it. We all know you and we know you hate doing something like this and it could never be your idea. But we want to keep you as our coach. So do it. What does it matter, anyway—captain shmaptain, big deal.

He let a good twenty seconds go by in silence, then said, You sure, Doober?

—I'm sure.

—Will it mess up the team very bad?

—Not at all. As you say, everyone will resent Nathan and hate her guts and her father's too, even more than before. But on the ice it won't make any difference.

—May I ask a favor? Of you?

—Maybe, I grouched.

—Just keep up your chatter, okay? You never needed the C to get your mouth open before, so don't let this, um, retraction shut you up. I depend on you talking out there. I know your feelings are hurt, or you're mad, or you're determined to get even somehow. But please—don't do it at the expense of my hockey team, of my guys. You yacked it up when Cody was captain. No reason to treat Nathan any different.

—There's one reason, I said.

—What's that?

—Cody's been my buddy since we were four and you got us all ice skates and took us out and taught us to play. So I knew Cody was a spacehead, and I knew *he* knew he was a spacehead, and would be grateful when I stuck my nose into his captain business.

—But Nathan you don't know.

—No. And it might be a little harder than usual getting to know her fast, if you get my meaning.

—You can always read *People* magazine. No— forget I said that. Sorry. Got it. Okay. Sorry.

—It's all right.

—Now, what are we going to do about Pincher?

—You mean his bad habits?

—Not only that, but I'm not even convinced yet

that he can clap his hands twice in a row. Does he have skills?

So I told him that yes, in fact Pincher did have some skills, including a dynamite shot from the point when he managed to stay there, and in fact when he did pinch and *get* the puck he destroyed the other team's defense by playing great in the circles, snapping a shot or backhanding a pass up the slot to the other D who was pinching too by now, for a one-timer. So Coach felt better about that.

I felt better about nothing.

three

One thing different about this Peewee year: The season started early and ended late. Two practices and suddenly we were getting dressed for our first game, one of two on a Saturday in early October.

The captain thing had worked out funny. While we were dressing for our second practice, before Coach Cooper even got a chance to arrive, Nathan stood on a bench and asked for everyone's attention, which, roughly, she got.

—Today Coach thinks he has to deliver a terrible piece of news to you, she said, a piece of news that tears him up and will make you furious. Since I am the cause of the news, if indirectly, and since I supposedly 'benefit' from it, though I am certain the opposite will be true, I might as well tell you myself. Here we go: This year the privilege of electing Dooby our captain—and he'd be the best one I can think of—instead of that, you are going to have another captain, *not* of your choosing, imposed upon you. That person will be me. I am going to be forced to be your captain, entirely because I am a girl and certain people think it would just be *so* neat to have a girl captain, and it's tough on everybody in this room. Resent me all you like. I can take it, as long as you still play hockey with me like anyone else when we're on the ice.

—Why don't you refuse? said Zip.

—My father would pull me from the team, and C or not, I love playing hockey, she said.

That was it. She started tightening her skates. There was silence, *big* silence. Then Coach Cooper walked in, and he was so caught up in phrasing his nasty news that he almost started speaking before he noticed he probably no longer had to.

—What happened? he asked Prince.

—Nathan just told us we got her as captain because she's a girl.

—That about sums it up, Coach said, looking curiously over at Nathan. Anybody want to say anything else?

—If I prove conclusively that I was born and raised on Uranus, said Zip, will someone think it would be neat to have a Uranian captain *next* year? I mean, I want a shot at glory too.

—Anybody else? said Coach Cooper. Okay. This is our last practice before two games on Saturday, so I want to set lines and defensive pairings. Also, I want to mention a few specific points: Nathan, hold your stick with both hands—skating around dragging it in one hand you look like a girl. Pincher, I want to see you shoot it from the point every time you get a chance. Woodsie, why is your swivel to the left suddenly so much slower than your swivel to the right? Didn't used to be, maybe you're not paying attention, fix it tonight. Dooby, I want you to try rushing the puck all the way through the neutral zone and across the blue line and into the freaking slot if they let you this year— your speed has really improved and people are giving you lots of ice, so take it. Barry, whatever happens out there, do not shoot. Questions? No, Zip, nothing from you. Anybody else? Okay. Ninety seconds.

The scrimmage went pretty well for everybody but me. I played like crap, half on purpose. It went *too* well, if you want to know how I felt about it.

It was as if Nathan had done some great brave thing and now it was just fine she was wearing the C instead of old Doober from way back when in yon days of yore. Nobody seemed particularly angry, nobody made sure to deck Nathan with a nasty check or two, nobody stood up and said, What about Dooby's rights? I was mad at the whole bunch. This was loyalty?

Prince even sang afterward. He always does unless there is some tragedy, so I guess he felt there was no tragedy.

The worst thing probably was that I could not show how bad I had wanted it, because of the whole play-it-cool, it's-taken-care-of thing, Yeah, I guess I'll do it. Taken care of? Ha. But I had to act like it was no big deal that this person was serving in *my* job just because I was a male and she was not. Nobody but Ernie even said anything to me. Ernie's parents are from South Boston, and originally from Ireland, I think, and although Ernie was born in Baltimore he has a slight brogue because his parents speak with almost no one outside of family. Anyway, not to treat him like some bar-fighting stereotype, but he does have the worst temper on the team, so *he*, at least, was steamed. He dropped down beside me on the bench after we finished and said, You got screwed, man.

—Yeah, well, whatever, I said, with my best imitation of an indifferent shrug.

—You don't have to pull that stuff with me, man. I can see you wanted it and that's cool, and we wanted you, too. We really did. These wussies in here acted like there was nothing wrong today but there *is* something wrong and I want you to know it will not be forgotten. A price will be paid.

—Hey, Ernie, I really appreciate the, like, sympathy, and you happen to be right about wanting it and being disappointed, but, like, I'd rather not murder Nathan in her sleep or anything. I mean, waiting for something like revenge is only going to hurt the—

—You don't be a wussy, too, okay? I'm not going to burn down the rink or anything, all right? Feel better? But a man can't let this crap just go by, you know? Because it won't stop, man. We'll start getting jobbed again and again, believe it. Unless we let some people know we noticed we were being jobbed, and we didn't like it very much. So, okay, I promise, no piano wire around the throat, right? But I'm with you, Doobs, and I want to see you get what you got coming. *All* of us do. It's just that most of us seem to have, like, lost our souls all of a sudden.

four

o, with all this stuff curling back on itself inside me, the hockey season started. The hockey season does not curl back on itself. It is like an arrow and once it leaves the bowstring it will keep going straight as long as it goes, game to game to game, and the best way to enjoy it—and to contribute to it— is to do the same. Always before, I have made myself ready, and the way I do that is by making sure that for one small time before the first game, like the arrow held on the string, I am completely still and clean and poised. I don't know where the season will take me, but I am ready to fly wherever it goes.

The one big way in which I differ from this arrow thing is that although I am still and set, I am *not* silent. Because being silent is not for me a means to concentrate, refine my energy, and narrow my focus, the way it is for most other people. For me, all that stuff comes from being still but also being very, very noisy.

But this year in the locker room as I sat with my energy all gathered and my concentration taut and my body ready to spring, I just had nothing to say; nothing came that made me open my mouth. It felt awful—I was empty. I was angry, but that left me with nothing. I had lost something mysterious and I did not know where to look. Anger did not replace it. Anger is not a *substance* the way that something you just have to say *is* a substance, pushing from inside, plucking its way up your throat in a prickly little hurry to get out. No, anger is different. Anger is a hole. It sucks things into itself and they are gone. That's why coaches try to motivate their teams by making them angry because of something—angry/loyal because a teammate just took a cheap shot from an opponent, or angry/shamed because they haven't been playing as hard as they can.

Cody noticed I was quiet and said something slight and jokey and off-the-mark about it; Woodsie was the only one who noticed and felt there might be more to it, there might be something wrong.

He sat down on the bench next to me. I had picked this small bench in the corner of the room to get dressed at, which was not my usual spot. Everybody else was being so excited and noisy, no one missed me out in the middle of it, except Woodsie, because all of a sudden from behind he stepped over the bench in his skates and sat down next to me.

—That's the first time I ever saw you take a seat in here, I said kind of halfheartedly.

—And that is the first sentence I have heard you speak today, he said, which is just as rare as my speaking as much as I am about to do. Personally, I hate sitting down. You do not play hockey sitting down, you do not live life sitting down, at least as a kid, and if you get in the habit of sitting down you find it harder and harder, stranger and stranger, to be at your best upright where you belong. Correct me if I'm wrong, but I suspect that if you gave it a thought you'd say you feel much the same about being *silent*, yes?

I shrugged. Belatedly, I said, Yeah, whatever.

—It worries me, he said, looking at me through the white grid of his face mask. I've been thinking, during these days when you've been less vocal, and I've realized how much I depend on you to say things as the game goes on. Some things that are constructive, some things that are useless except for being funny or stupid or inspiring or hotheaded. I don't want to lay too much on you, no burden here, no undeserved responsibility—but your talk is the breath of our games.

—Gee, that's pretty, I said. Then I sighed, and managed to say, Better get a respirator for today.

—Nothing to say, huh?

I shook my head.

—Don't think it will come, the chattering and all that, once you hit the ice for real?

I shook my head again. No way, I said. Nobody home inside.

He nodded as if it was just what he had expected. You're paired with Barry, right?

—Right.

—Who is himself no source of spoken wisdom.

—No, he's pretty quiet. But we know each other well enough we don't need to say much to cover what we need to.

—That's what I thought, Woodsie said. And that

takes care of your personal job as a defenseman on the ice, which, as you and Barry are our top pair of defensemen, is undeniably important. But I'm more concerned about the rest of it—what your incredibly productive mouth provides for everyone else *but* Barry, who doesn't really need it.

I shrugged again. Then I pointed across the room with my stick. That's the kind of inspiration you're supposed to get from your captain.

Woodsie looked along my stick at Nathan.

He said nothing, so I pressed it. Am I right? All that talk, all that *noticing* and *then* talking, the words you're referring to, inspiring and instructive—that nice 'breath.' There's where you're supposed to get it. Right?

He got up, standing tall beside me, and let out a long sigh. Then he dropped a hand onto my shoulder pad. Okay, he said. You can shut up now.

—But I thought you wanted—

—You know what I wanted. And you know where we're not going to get it. But if you've got any extra breath in there, and words, don't waste them being mean.

—I'm just a defenseman, I said. I skate my shifts.

—Well, he said, at least you're good at that. Kind of formally, very Woodsie-like, he added, Have a good game, Teammate. Then he stepped back over the bench and was gone.

I did not have a good game. It was not a *bad* game—I played well, actually; my shift only allowed two shots on Zip all day, and I personally broke up two odd-man rushes with killer sweep-checks at just the right moment. Barry and I did our usual grunting and pointing and mind-reading so that one of us was always hassling after the puck and other was making sure the slot stayed clear of anyone getting set up to shoot or tip the puck if it happened to whiz his way.

But I never said a word. It was weird—in the course of the game I sat there and noticed all these times I *would* have said something if it had been there inside, times like when a Bowie defensemen stuck his stick between Prince's legs and jacked him two feet into the air just as Prince was about to pounce on a rebound with the Bowie goalie lying on his belly facing the other way and there was no call, or times like the shifts in which Ernie and Pincher, who had never played together, kept failing to talk and divide the work by saying who would chase and who would stay home. At least three times they both went after the puck in the corner, leaving the slot full of Bowie dudes, and all three times the puck came across and Zip got smoked, twice on rebounds, once on the *third* rebound, which is a disgrace.

I noticed that the idea came to me to talk to Coach and suggest that he switch Pincher to wing and drop Java back to D in his place. It would have been a brilliant suggestion: Java is extremely conservative, he rarely takes advantage of his speed or his great hands or his talent for hitting, because he is thinking ahead of how this or that move might leave the team vulnerable, while Pincher, of course, plays the opposite—recklessly offensive, focused only on the puck and the moment. In other words, Java thinks like a natural defenseman, and Pinch non-thinks like a natural puck-hound scorer.

But I didn't speak to the coach about it.

Four times Cody tried to swing wide on this one defenseman who backskated too fast for him, and every time he rode Codes into the boards. But I noticed the kid got all his backspeed from huge, pretty, clinic-demonstration-worthy crossovers, always the same leg crossing, and it just so happened that crossing this way would have left him helplessly six feet out of Cody's way and headed further off if only Codes had cut *inside* one of those rushes, and he would have had a clean stroll down the slot and almost certainly would have scored. Cody can fool almost any goalie in close and his variety of shots is awesome but this goalie happened to be pretty weak and *very* nervous. Boot ate him alive, scoring on consecutive shifts in the first, until the Bowie coach put one defenseman on him as a shadow and had his winger on that side play way back to double the Boot and we never heard from him again. Shark got one by giving the puck to Woodsie at the blue line and then simply busting through everything in his path, including his own center, until he found himself six feet from the goalie and the puck suddenly showed up on his stick blade, courtesy of Woodsie who had just held it. The goalie's skates were twenty inches apart and his stick was four inches off the ice.

Unfortunately, so was Nathan's much of the time and I would have said so to her if I were playing my normal game. Three beautiful centering passes from Kenny, to launch each of which he took a beating from a double- and one time a *triple*-teaming, skittered harmlessly beneath her blade and it was all wasted. Her lifted blade is just one of those things, almost all players have something like that, a habit they need to be reminded of. I'm always the guy who reminds them. But not today. Maybe not anymore, period. Who knows?

We won anyway, even though they slightly outplayed us, because we had our secret nuclear warhead, Kenny. He scored three goals, all in the third period, the last with less than a minute left and both of his skates in the air behind him from a stone-dead hook the ref had not raised his hand to call on the defender whose stick blade was still crossing both of K's boots three feet above the ice, and we won 6–5. Don't get me wrong, I like having K back at Wolfbay after his year away on the failed Montrose 'super-team.' But through the years I have never liked depending on Kenny to work some miracles and pull us out of the fire. I'd rather we played well enough to have a one-goal lead all by ourselves and *then* let Kenny cut loose and make it a five-goal victory.

One thing happened that made me realize how differently I must be projecting myself. I may not have mentioned it, but Kenny and I are about the same height, though I weigh about fifteen pounds more than him, and we both wear JOFA helmets, and our shoulder pads are the same kind. Well, as we were jamming in a bunch through the gate off the ice I felt a hard poke from behind and heard Shark say, Hey, Kenny, couldn't you score one under *challenging* circumstances once in a while?

I turned my head and Shark saw who I was and said, Oh, sorry, Doobs, I thought—

—No problem, I said.

But anytime someone can mistake me, Doobermouth—as Zip calls me sometimes—for the quietest, shyest kid in the state, there *is* a problem. There *must* be.

five

nd here we are two days later, ten minutes from game time, and I do not feel one bit better, do not have one thing to say. In his remarks before warm-ups, Coach gives this little speech about looking for leadership from our leaders and he stares at me hard. And from that speech he goes straight to a description of my new "privileges" just to make everything nice and clear: Doobs is getting something, so don't we have the right to expect maybe he should give something, too?

Yes, all right, I'm supposed to start performing every defenseman's dream: carrying the puck, even deep into the offensive zone if possible, whoopee! Of course, a defenseman who rushes the puck is not just having fun, he's opening himself and his team up to all kinds of perilous reversals—the deeper he lugs the ol' rubber into his zone, the farther he takes himself out of his defensive position, which is back at the blue line, behind everyone else, ready to back up and stay between his puck-bearing opponent and the cage defended by his goalie. Instead, if the defenseman-playing-offense loses the puck, he finds himself watching the backs of the people he is supposed to be on the other side of, as they zoom in on his underprotected goalie two-on-one or three-on-two.

True, the coach *told* me to start trying this risky style of play, so technically I am excused from humiliations that might accrue. But of course, being excused from personal shame is not what this is about; giving up goals that add up to more than we score ourselves—*that's* what it's about. Losing sucks, even when you have a note from Coach exonerating you.

And of course, having spent the past two weeks silently counting the number of teammates who did not think to call and offer any sort of condolences, or to snarl in anger along with me, or just to check and make sure ol' Doober-woober was taking this reverse-discrimination thing okay, having spent all that time chewing on my indignation mostly in private (no one called but Cody, his dad,

Prince, and, strangely, because he had nothing to say but managed to make me feel all warm-and-fuzzy anyway, Kenny Moseby), I am still dead inside, as in the first game. I do not feel ready to go out and get aggressive and play high-stakes-black-jack-hockey. I feel as if I *might* be able to get by doing the minimum of ultraconservative defensive play and basically hiding behind my very dependable partner Barry.

Coach reminds me one last time to 'take it to 'em.' He also reminds Nathan to hold her stick hard and bend it to the ice (what kind of a travel Peewee needs to be told something so basic?), and instructs both Prince and Pinch to pepper the Reston goalie with shots, shots, shots, generating rebounds, rebounds, rebounds.

Speaking of rebounds, Shark's composure and aggressiveness are nice surprises. He started last year as a total incompetent but improved at rushing the net. He decided to take his improvement seriously. He went to five hockey camps this summer, he's gained twenty more pounds, he looks immovable if he plants his butt in the slot. And of course, our most opportunistic goal scorer, the Boot, also loves those rebounds. There is no one in either of our two leagues who can get his stick on the puck— even just a tiny flick—as quickly and sneakily as the Boot. There will be a shot, a save, the puck tumbling toward the ice in the middle of five or six guys packed into a few cubic feet, all with sticks and hands and skates, and somehow before the puck has even really hit the ice it is behind the goalie. Score one for the Boot, and never mind how he weaseled his stick through all the legs and sticks and skates to give the rubber just the snap it needed to pop it between the goalie's blocker pad and his torso. . . .

Next thing I know, we're warming up, little shooting drills I can never remember doing because, usually, as soon as my skates touch ice my mouth starts running, and I pass the whole warmup time in a wild scatter of chatter, making what seem like very important points to this person and then dropping him halfway to spin and catch another guy and start telling *him* something I wanted to be sure he realized, at least until a third guy skates by and I remember, oh *yes!*, that I absolutely had to tell him this very critical thing about the man he most likely will be checking. . . .

But today, once again, I am not chattering. Instead, I am noticing the dippy little shooting drill and messing up every time I get the puck. Cody says, Come on, man—wake up and wake *us* up! but I can't climb out of my sulk. Coach calls out the starters. Naturally, since I am barely aware, I am one of them.

Then the game starts.

Reston is always a team of very large guys, for some reason; fortunately, they are usually also pretty slow and not all that nifty with the stick-handling. I can usually count on ten or fifteen poke checks against Reston, *effortless* poke checks. So today their center wins the draw and a defenseman hits the left wing with a pass as the winger crosses the blue line on my side, and I'm backskating with my skates a little wide because of course I'm about to poke this dude and I want to have my weight forward to jump into my first rush.

The only trouble is that I give the dude my poke, but he has curled the puck wide to the boards-side and I miss it, then as I lunge at it he neatly pulls it back so it passes right beneath my nose as I plunge full-speed onto the ice and into the boards. By the time I get to my knees I hear behind me that he has beaten Zip and scored. Great. Zip will be furious for a month about this one goal; if they get another, it will be two months. Zip hates to open the game by falling behind, especially when it's not really his fault. All goalies are born blamers, and sometimes they are right.

—Sorry, Zip, I say in a dull, low voice that doesn't sound anything like me, even after I have messed up. Zip notices, and stops the insult that was on his lips long enough to say, Hey, are you, like, *alive* or in some other state?

—I don't know, I say, but by then the insults have resumed, and I skate away from them, back for the center-ice face-off, with a revised opinion of the stickhandling skills of at least the left wing. Barry whacks me on the seat of my pants with his stick, a gesture of support and solidarity. Where was the solidarity when my C got ripped off by someone whose sole qualification was the lack of a Y chromosome?

This time Prince wins the face-off and the puck comes rolling on its edge exactly between Barry and me. Either of us could collect it, but we both hold back for a second or two, expecting the other to reach for it, and then in a panic we both lunge at it as it rolls, but we have waited half a second too long. The same Reston winger has darted onto the puck and knocked it past us and followed it fast to bear in on poor Zip as Barry and I, sticks extended directly at each other's pants, jam right into each other.

The winger scores, a dead breakaway off a face-off we won. Barry's eyes are about eight inches from mine; we have gotten tangled somehow, and just stand there yanking and pushing and trying to get free.

—That was it, Barry says, as Coach hollers Change! and we head for the bench. The people coming onto the ice swing *way* wide of the two of us so they won't even have to make eye contact.

—That was what? I ask.

—That was my worst moment in hockey up to now. That was the bottom. That was the lowest, the most inexcusably lame—

—And I'm proud to have shared it with you, Bare. I slide onto the bench.

—Tough luck on the roll, Coach says over his shoulder.

—Nice of you to say so, I reply. And what about that *really* tough luck on the full embrace of two defensemen facing away from the play? It was a complex little moment and I thought we managed rather well, getting tangled up like that so quick when, hey, we haven't even *practiced* it.

—Shut up, Dooby, says the Boot's voice calmly off to my right.

—Righto, Bootster.

—No, says the Coach. Don't shut up. Sorry, Boot. Keep talking, Doober. Tell us—tell us what you felt, deep in the tenderest places of your hockey heart, when you entered Barry's eagerly opened arms.

—Well, I start—but nothing else comes. Watching his back, I can feel the coach waiting for my mouth to engage, *wanting* it even, but it does not happen. I am shocked and nervous at my own silence, but I just don't *feel* it. I keep seeing Nathan and her C. Twice now our "Captain" failed to get in the face of the linesmen on a couple of bogus offside calls. I keep wondering why I used to get so involved in these games, I keep just watching Zip make save after save without getting myself in the least riled that our D is allowing so many quality shots.

When it's our shift I make a special effort, and ask the Reston left wing what his middle name is just as the ref drops the puck, and the kid wrinkles his forehead for just an instant, his lips forming the M sound that would lead to a question about his middle name and my strange curiosity about it, and by then he's out of the play. Prince has won the face-off and pulled the puck back to Barry, who skates it one stride over the red line and whistles it in high along the boards, a classic hard-around. I tear for the far point, watching as the goalie goes behind the cage to try to stop the puck for his defensemen standing there but he can't get it. I reach the point, one foot inside the blue line, half a second before the puck suddenly dies and drops off the boards, landing at my feet. My arms were already in their backswing, and on a hunch I launch a tremendous swing that carries my stick blade about four inches above the surface of the ice. My hunch was right: the puck had a little bounce left in it, and I catch it fat, perfect, home run from the instant it leaves the bat. My follow-through is a nice two-footed spin that just brings the cage into my field of vision as the puck disappears through some gap in the goalie's hastily assembled facade.

It is definitely a hot goal.

I turn toward Zip and point my stick at him. He slips off his catching glove and holds up one *more* finger, as if to say that I haven't made up for my bad plays yet. Then my teammates are battering me and giving Barry a load of grief because he will undoubtedly pick up the assist and he hates to have anything to do with scoring.

We change up. As I skate by the wing, I know I would usually put the stake through his heart with the perfect whizz of words. But today, though I just fooled him and scored a great goal, I go suddenly flat, and coming up with a cut seems like too much trouble. I tuck my chin and head to the bench.

—Good whack, Doober, says Coach.

—Very fine release, says the Boot, a more discerning critic.

—Great goal, mumbles Kenny Moseby as he passes me on his way onto the ice.

Then there's this catch at my sleeve that won't let go, and I tug against it, and it still holds, and I turn to see if I've snagged my sweater on the bench door or something, but then I see it's the grip of a hockey glove, and I follow the sleeve up to the helmet, and I see Nathan.

—Nice, she says.

—Thanks.

Then she skates out.

This is a strange line Coach has put together: Sandy Beckstein at center, with Moseby and Nathan on the wings. When he announced it the other day, of course I just fed it into the flames of my anger: not only did she get to be captain, but she also got to play on Moseby's line! Perfect! What's next— a percentage of the skate-sharpening concession?

However, as I watch them play as if from about a mile away, I think I can begin to see what Coach had in mind. Sandy is a bulldog for the puck and a smart if not especially creative passer; he will also shoot without hesitation if he's in close, even from a bad angle—for some reason, he's very good at those flat-angle shots. Kenny, of course, can receive even the sloppiest pass and turn it into an assist with a flick of the wrist from anywhere. And Nathan can zip around the circles looking adroit and dangerous even if she isn't. On offense, it's a nightmare to defend against.

Defensively, Beckstein is once again very tenacious and responsible; the guys he checks never get away from him for very long, if at all. In fact, he is so tenacious that Zip decided "Subtle" would be a perfect nickname for our team's elder skatesman. Kenny is basically another super-responsible checker, with the save-the-day genius potential I mentioned earlier. Nathan is terrible at physically engaging anybody—guys just brush her off, and it isn't because she is slight or anything: She's way bigger than Kenny and Cody and even a little bigger than the new meaty Prince. No, the reason she's lousy at physically challenging another player is just that she really doesn't care, doesn't like the contact, gives it up easily. So she's useless as a defender except in one way: She can catch up to anyone on a breakaway from behind. So Coach has Kenny and Sandy playing pretty deep D for forwards, well inside the face-off dots—and if having them so low allows an opposing forward to cherry-pick and get away for a break, then Nathan gets to do her speed thing. Once she catches her prey, he is coming in on goal so fast she only has to mess with the guy's stick for a second or give his glove a little tug-hook and that will be enough, he'll be past the moment when he could shoot.

As it happens, this morning the Beckstein line is the only one that is not scored upon. So I guess Coach's idea was okay.

The game started wide open—two goals on the first shift is pretty weird—and it stays that way. Unfortunately for Reston, anytime you play a wide-open game against Kenny Moseby you are going to come up short. Moze gets four goals for himself—all in the second period—and sets up various teammates for a bunch of others. Woodsie got one on a nice lifted backhander, I think Prince had one, maybe Shark too. . . . In any case, we win, 9–3. Zip plays great, makes some out-of-his-mind saves and shuts them out in the third period when they pull out all the stops and put an incredible nineteen shots on him.

We all know it was a pretty lousy victory, whatever the score. Too many great saves required of Zip, too many marvels required of Kenny. It did not feel good to be out there with each other. Guess who needs to get onto that problem and find a way to inspire its fixin'? That's right: Calling Captain Nathan!

My goal loosened me up for a few minutes, but I played most of the game as a stiff, a very quiet stiff. As for Nathan, she didn't talk either, even though there were three obvious times she ought to have said something, *any*thing, to the ref, just to show somebody on our side was watching and gave a hoot. She almost seemed to shy away from two of these opportunities, skating off with her head down. Some captain.

After the game, before getting from the ice to the locker room, I did finally get to meet the famous namesake of the Widgeon Award himself—Nathan's father, the man behind the plan to put Wolfbay on the tabloid reader's map. He didn't come to practices—I'm sure Nathan told him that might be a little too much like rubbing it in—but he was certainly a big presence at the game. He's about 6'4, 210, with hair the color of Tang breakfast drink powder and lots of it, sweeping up and backward off his forehead in tight waves. His eyes are too small for his size but they are a startling green color and they contain a world of suspicion that some people might mistake for the flash of intelligence. He tried to introduce himself to each of us as we bunched through the gate off the ice, but nobody really responded, even though he knew every player's name but mine flawlessly.

I was unlucky: He grabbed me, and stuck his face close into mine—I vowed never to take my helmet off again until I was out of his sight—and said, Pretty decent recovery after that disastrous first shift. Boy, what a joke *that* was.

—Glad you were amused, I said, and pulled my arm free.

—Hey, I didn't mean—

—Maybe you didn't *mean*, I snapped over my shoulder, and half-turned. But you *said*, didn't you? You said it was a *joke*. Well, listen up, Pops—we aren't *ever* joking out there.

—You're making a big mistake, son—I think you'll find I'm a *very* sophisticated watcher and analyst of—

—I won't 'find' anything, I said, because I

don't care enough to look.

I turned and walked on. A few steps later he called after me.

—What was your name?

—Joe Hardy, I said. And my brother Frank plays center. Then I made it to the locker room. Inside the door I stood for a second, taking a look. It was a pretty happy place—Zip and Cody were hollering something harmless at each other, Barry had one naked foot and one foot with the skate still on, tied tight, and he was staring with a typical grumpy look into his bag while keeping track of some argument Prince and Java were having about music. As usual, Woodsie was floating behind the action, inserting a barb here and there, and as usual Ernie was trying to laugh at everything everybody said. I noticed Pincher was looking pretty relaxed as he gabbled at Shinny, who had his cast almost entirely inside somebody's bag. Beckstein was undressing alone and smiling to himself, looking very satisfied.

I did not feel the way these people felt. I felt robbed. I had scored a nice goal, made some good plays late in the game to atone a little for my first-shift goofs, but I couldn't hold the game in my mind, even on the ice—so what hope did I have of carrying any joy over into the locker room?

Nevertheless, I had to change clothes, so I sort of snuck between people to where my bag lay.

I had both skates off and was pulling my sweater over my head before I remembered I had not looked for our noble captain. I scanned the room and didn't see her; then I dropped my gaze lower, and this time I saw her. She was sitting on a bench, leaning forward, with her chin in both hands, still in her full uniform, doing nothing but staring at the wall. I kept checking on her the whole time it took me to change. She never moved.

Later in the day we won again, a tight one, 3–1, and she got a goal. Her father, banging on the glass, communicated by sign language to the ref that he would like to have the puck she had shot in. It took a while, but the ref eventually understood, and skated up to the glass and flipped the biscuit over it. Nathan's father caught it, brushed it off with a swipe of his hand, blew on it, held it up toward the stands, and waved it back and forth. He didn't seem to notice that nobody was looking. Then he put the puck in his coat pocket and went for a stroll through the spectators, speaking to most of them. Wonder what he was calling their attention to?

I looked down the bench at Nathan. To my huge surprise, she was crying. Making no attempt to stifle or hide it, just crying softly away, tears running out around the sides of her chinstrap.

I had to admit the C on her sweater didn't seem to be much comfort right then.

I suppose I could have said Nice goal! or something. It never crossed my mind. I'd like to say I intuited that right then she would have given anything *not* to have jammed in that rebound of Kenny's shot, and that I was sensitive enough to avoid the whole topic. But it's not true. I was not feeling sensitive. I hate to admit it, but I sat there and I enjoyed her crying. Keep it up, I said in my head, cry forever, cry long enough that nobody ever wants to give you anything just because you're a girl again.

Just keep crying, I pleaded, silently, inside myself, where it hurt the most.

six

I was dreaming something about trying to play hockey in the sand at the beach, and instead of pucks we were using these little metal balls with very sharp spikes on them, and no one wanted to take a shot because it was obvious these things could kill a goalie. Then I was lying on my back in the sand shaking like crazy, and then, finally, I realized my mom was shaking me awake.

—It's dark, I said.

—Your coach is downstairs. He wants to see you.

I jumped out of bed and started to move toward my closet, but then I realized I had no reason to assume I should get dressed. If Coach Cooper came calling in the middle of the night he must expect to see some pajamas. So I just stuck my feet in an old pair of loafer Vans and followed my mom downstairs.

Coach was in the living room, still standing up, feet apart, watching for us. He was dressed in jeans and a parka and boots. His boots looked wet.

I sniffed. Smoke, I said.

—Even worse, said the Coach. Fire.

—What—

—Nothing bad, he said. Somebody torched a pile of pucks on Nathan's sidewalk about an hour ago. Also the person scratched the word *pig* on the hood, the trunk lid, and each of the two doors of her dad's car. Scratched it *deep*, probably with a diamond drill bit.

—What kind of car? I asked. It was a stupid question, but I didn't know what was going on and I had been asleep three minutes ago.

—A Miata.

—They're little, I said, then yawned. Coach nodded. His expression was very tired, but also very alert. The letters are big, though. *P-I-G*.

—Big Pig, I said, like it was a joke, which it was not.

He just stared at me for a few moments, then let out a little sigh.

—How many pucks? I asked.

—About twenty. Probably still burning. Stinking mess.

—Nobody hurt? The puck fire didn't spread to, like, Nathan's house or anything?

He shook his head. The father lives in a rented townhouse, he said for some reason.

—The father lives—oh, you mean, like, the parents are separated or something?

He nodded.

—Was Nathan staying at his place tonight?

He nodded.

—Is—I tried to think of what I wanted to ask, but all I came up with was, Is she very upset?

He let out a long breath of air. Yes, he said. She is extremely upset.

I still don't know why the next thing popped out, but out of nowhere I said, Don't let her quit.

He frowned at me. How did you know she wanted to quit?

—Pretty easy. She blames herself for sure. She gets made captain, people build up resentments—

I stopped dead, remembering my talk with Ernie and his vague threats. My eyes must have gone kind of inward, because Coach could tell I was remembering something.

—Do you have any idea who was building up a resentment like that, Doobs? Has anybody told you anything?

—You think I wouldn't say something if somebody told me he was going to trash a car, set even a small fire? I was acting angry; it hid my confused thoughts pretty well. You think I'd protect somebody like that, let it happen, maybe get somebody hurt—

—Okay, okay, take it easy, I wasn't suggesting anything that definite.

—Well, good.

We both just stood there for a minute. Then he sighed and said, The trouble is, I haven't seen anyone giving her a hard time at all. Pardon me for mentioning it, and don't think for a second that I suspected you, but—well, really, you're the only one on the team whose behavior has changed radically.

—It has? I said, pretending to be incredulous. Radically?

—Let's just say you have been less than happy

and chatty. We might add that you've been acting a little like someone who feels he has a righteous grudge.

—Look, I started. But he shook his head.

—I told you—not for a second.

I nodded. It was pretty weird to think people noticed me being quieter so much. Suddenly I was very ashamed.

—Did you think you could stop all that noise and no one would notice?

—I wasn't *trying* to be quiet, I said. It's just, nothing was there.

—It's okay, he said. I'm not worried. Nothing can shut you up forever.

—Don't bet on it.

—I guess we'll see, he said. Well, if you're sure you don't have any ideas about who might be this mad—

—None, I said.

He nodded, then said, I'll be going then. He took a few steps toward the door, nodding good night to us.

—Are you going back to—back there? Where the, um, damage was?

He stopped. Well, he said, as a matter of fact I am. Why?

I shrugged. I don't know, I said. I guess—I hope, like, Nathan is okay and all.

—Want to come? he said.

I looked at my mom. She said, Go ahead if you want to. She could probably use someone to be with.

And she'll be thrilled it's *me*, I thought, as I hopped upstairs and pulled on some clothes. When I came down again, my mom said Coach was waiting in his truck, so I ran out through the dark and jumped into the front seat when he swung the door open from inside.

—You sure you're up to this? Coach asked, studying me.

I nodded. I think I just got over the captain thing, I said. I looked out of the window as we passed dark house after dark house. Jeez, I blurted, I mean, *pig* four times!

—It's possible this has nothing to do with the team, Coach said. Don't forget, this guy is a royal jerk. Worth at *least* four reps of the term of your choice. He must have plenty of enemies.

—It's the hockey, I said, and wished I hadn't.

—How can you be sure? What do you know, Dooby?

—Nothing, I said. I don't know anything. It's just a feeling, that's all. I mean—I guess I was taking it too seriously, for *me*. So I can kind of see somebody else taking it too seriously, only, like, it must be somebody who's—well, who's—

—Who's destructive, Coach finished for me.

I shivered. I guess maybe some people feel, like, threatened or something. Like maybe this is the start of a trend to take things away from guys and give them to girls or something.

He laughed. If that's what they're worried about, they're at least fifteen years behind the times in most areas of human life.

Both of us knew what that meant: This must be a kid who hadn't seen anything like this happen before, because his dad didn't have a job in an office or complain about lost bids for city contracts or whatever. A kid who got his first look at things when they happened to his hockey team.

Come to think of it, that described most of us.

We pulled around a corner and there it was, the

scene of the crime. It was very disappointing—just this little car with flares stuck around it, sputtering so you could barely read the simple word dug into the four surfaces. Nathan's dad was standing there in a robe with wingtips on and no socks, holding a bunch of unlit flares; beside him, looking very bored, was a little guy with a notepad, probably with PIG written down four times, and that was about it for the crime. While we drove up, a flare spluttered out and Nathan's father sadly replaced it with a fresh one, so he wouldn't have to stop contemplating the horror of his stupid scratched car.

The puck fire was just a smoldering ooze that didn't even go all the way across the sidewalk.

—Anyway, it's *his* fault, not hers, I said just before we got out. I didn't see Nathan anywhere.

—What?

—The whole thing wasn't *her* idea, it was *his*, I said. Or the board's, or whatever. But she didn't even want it.

—When did you get all this info? he asked, not getting out yet.

—When she told us that day. Before you could. You remember.

He thought for a minute. Think carefully and try to recall as clearly as you can: Did she say specifically that it was her father's doing?

—I think so. I don't know—we'd been talking about him anyway, or Sandy and Pinch had. About how he used to help her get suited up and how she hated it. She said something like, He doesn't think I can take a breath unless he's there to supervise.

Coach nodded. And do you remember who was in the room at the time? At both times?

I shrugged. The team. The guys.

—The guys, he repeated. Then he opened his door and I opened mine. Nathan's dad and the other man nodded at Coach Coop, then stared at me.

—Dooby's a hockey buddy of Kathy's, Coach said. He asked if she was upset, and whether she might like some company.

—Try the kitchen, said her dad, without a hello or a Thanks for coming or anything. He just kept staring at the words on his little car and shaking his head. A couple of times he said, Nine thousand miles. That's all—nine thousand.

—I'll try the kitchen, I said.

Only one of the townhouses had lights on inside, and what looked like the only door to the place was standing wide open. I knocked on the open door and said, Hello? There was no answer. Looking in, I could see a light coming down a hallway from the rear of the house. I decided that was probably the kitchen, and walked on in.

The hallway was short, and it emptied me into a small kitchen that had a high island table in the middle, with three barstools around it. Nathan was sitting on one of the stools, leaning forward on her elbows, flipping something black that rolled back and forth from hand to hand on the countertop. Beside her a very large bowl of vanilla ice cream was melting.

She looked up, at the same moment that I realized the black thing was the puck her father had made such a big deal of retrieving.

—Yo the Doobster, she said.

—Hi, Nathan.

—Want some ice cream?

—No, thanks.

She was wearing a big T-shirt with Kurt Cobain's

face on it and old jeans blown out at the knees and a pair of red canvas sneakers. She batted the puck a couple more times, then straightened up with a sigh. She took the puck in her right hand and scaled it across the room into a little alcove where I saw a washer and dryer.

—So what brings you to the conflagration? she asked, looking at me in quick glances.

—I thought you might need somebody to keep you from getting any stupid ideas.

—Oh? she said, with a small smile. Such as?

—Such as thinking any of this is your fault, or is directed against you, or should be taken personally in any way. And such as thinking any dumb thoughts about not staying on the team.

—You know what? I got this *call*, this *phone* call, from some lady at some national organization dedicated to making sure women engaged in 'groundbreaking' activities were guaranteed their rights and full protection. She was very aggressive. She just would not get the idea through her head that I was not some gutsy pioneer but, quite the contrary, was just another female being used as a Cute Chick by a bunch of guys.

—That's right, I said. Remember, this wasn't your idea. So you're not the one who's responsible, or the one who's resented.

—What do you mean? You yourself resent me terribly. I stole your job. You hate my guts.

—No, I said. I do not. I never did; it wasn't you, yourself, at all. I actually like you a lot; everybody on the team does, and if you think about it you know it's true. It's also true, yes, I was being stupid, and I did resent what happened.

—You resented *me*, she said. You can say it; it's okay. I'll let you take it back.

—Okay. I resented you *and* the whole setup. It was a mistake to make you captain for the reason they did, but I've been kind of a jerk about it. I was wrong. I also respected you, and I was right to do that.

—Because I'm a pioneer? she said.

—Because you're my teammate, and you work hard, and I know that if it came down to it you would stand up for me, and I would stand up for you. And by the way, it was a nice goal, and whatever happened after doesn't change that.

She sat there thinking for a minute, then said,

Okay, but why shouldn't I quit?

—Because it's too late to quit. You're on the team, you're on a good line, and, for whatever reason, you're the captain and your teammates other than me have done a perfect job of getting behind you.

She started playing with the spoon sticking out of the ice cream, dribbling lumpy little streams off it into the bowl.

—My father's car was a piece of crap before this, she said. I actually think the new decorations add some character. But it's still too small for him—he looks like some fat lady trying to fit her huge feet into a pair of dainty little size fives.

—Zip says Miatas are midlife-crisis cars for people who don't have the guts to get what they want, which—

—is a Corvette. He's right. She laughed briefly. I like Zip. She jammed the spoon into the ice cream and put her face into her hands for about two seconds, then said, That's the problem—I like *all* of you guys. Even you, Mr. Sulky Redass.

—Why don't you just set a number, so I know how many times I have to apologize before—

—It's over already, you're done, we're palsy-walsies for life, no bad stuff left. Okay, she said. I won't quit.

—Cool! I smiled.

She looked at me and laughed. What's 'cool' about it?

—I actually had a positive effect on another human being at a moment of crisis, I said. I'm, like, a psychology-stud.

—No; you're, like, a person who vastly overrates his powers, but never mind. I appreciate you coming over.

—I would hope so. Your dad was too lost in mourning to even say hello. 'Nine thousand miles!' Like he can't even drive it anymore.

She laughed. What a bozo. And it was more like 9,700 anyway. She shot me a look. So who did it, Doobs?

I kind of jumped. I—

—You must have some idea. You're the injured party. Whoever it was must have been drooling all over you in your victimhood at some point.

—I don't know, I said, a little more firm-sounding than I wanted.

She shrugged. Whatever, she said. It's your conscience.

—No, I said. It's not my conscience at all. I was home in bed.

—Got it, she said. You didn't set the actual pucks on fire or scratch the Miata, so you're completely clean, right? No knowledge or ideas count, of course.

—I'm out of here, I said, turning back toward the front door. Glad you didn't get hurt, and kiss my butt.

—Thanks, Dooby. I mean it.

—Just be there for the next practice, I said. I walked out. As soon as he saw me, Coach Cooper separated from the two other guys, who hadn't moved, and came and put his arm around my shoulder.

—How is she?

—Fine. She's not quitting.

He squeezed my shoulder. We said good-night to the two men. I couldn't help noticing that unlike her hockey coach, Nathan's father didn't ask how she was. He just stared and shook his head and replaced the flares. Just before we pulled away I rolled down my window and said to the little man with the notebook, Hey—I'd check the insurance angle *very* closely if I were you. Coach laughed and cussed and peeled out of there fast.

—Why . . . never mind.

—He's a weenie, I said.

—Even weenies shouldn't get their cars scratched up.

—At least it wasn't a 'Vette, I said.

rnie avoids me for the morning at school, but at lunch I slip into line behind him and take his elbow.

—Let's go talk, I say.

—I didn't do it, man.

—Do what, Ernie?

He looks at me, lips pressed, then nods and leaves the line with me. While everyone else eats, we go out onto the blacktop and keep walking until we're in the far corner, behind some climbing structures the little kids use.

—Okay, I say. Let's hear it.

He's very nervous. I'm really sorry, man. I didn't know anything would happen.

—What *did* happen?

He looks at me, drops his eyes, flicks his glance through about 240 degrees around us, wipes his mouth with a hand, and says, All right, man. It's like this. I got this cousin.

—What's his name?

—You don't want to know, okay? At least for the moment. We'll call him Mack. Mack, he's visiting from Boston. He's older than us, nineteen or twenty. Mack moved out on his own a couple of years ago and he's, like, gotten involved in some stuff, you know? Nothing too bad, but—well, bad enough.

—Do his parents know? Do yours?

He shakes his head, looks around again. No. Because he's got a job, a good job, something with computers, everybody's very proud, he wears fine clothes, he keeps up with the family. Like visiting down here—that's not what a tough guy does, spends a week with his aunt and uncle, you know?

—So, you go home the day we had our talk and you keep talking.

He nods. That's it, that's just what I do. I'm, like, fired up, man—I got a temper, and it doesn't just show itself in explosions. Sometimes it just keeps me a little short of the boil for *days*, and after starting to let some of it out with you I'm talking to myself all the way home and when I get back, nobody's there but Mack, and I guess I am acting pretty strange. So he says, like, What's up? What's the problem?

—So you tell him, about the board and the father forcing things.

—Right. And he just listens and nods, and then he sits and thinks. And I saw it come into his eyes, like a smile. I knew he was thinking he'd do something, something pretty harmless, nobody would get hurt, but—well, it's like he couldn't help wanting to just leave a little statement before he went home.

—He went home?

Ernie nods. This morning. Back to Boston. And if you got any ideas about trying to find him, forget it. He could disappear for as long as you kept looking.

—Did he tell you what he was going to do?

—Are you crazy? You think I'd sit back and let him scrape some guy's car? You think *anybody* would? No. But I saw that little eye-smile, and I told him I didn't want any trouble, I was just spouting off, it wasn't serious, please don't do anything. But it was too late. See, to him, the Nathan thing is just another piece of injustice added to thousands. To him, a big-city kid, it's all hooked up and it's evil.

I think for a minute. Ah, of course. He came to our games.

Ernie nods. Right. That was, like, one of the reasons for his visit, why he picked this particular weekend, so he could watch his little cousin play this Beantown sport. And, well, you saw what happened at the second game, with the father and the puck and all. That guy's a real butthole, I got to say.

—So Mack figured out Papa was the problem—

—I'd already told him something like that, from what Nathan and Coach told us.

—Right. So he follows Papa out to the car, maybe even follows him home. Then, last night, he leaves his message.

Ernie swings through another panorama check-out of the blacktop. Kids have started coming out of the lunchroom, but they're still far away.

—Yeah, well, nobody got hurt at least, Ernie says.

—Did he tell you?

Ernie shakes his head. Not a word, man. But I had a feeling, especially after that fool pulled the puck business.

—Why didn't you warn Nathan? I mean, he *did*

set a pile of pucks on fire. It was a small fire, but it was still dangerous.

He looks me in the eye for a long moment. Then, in a more composed voice, he says, First, I never thought he'd do a fire. Second, there are a lot of reasons and I'll spell them out if you want, and I bet some of them are the same reasons you probably kept your earlier talk with me to yourself. But first let me ask you: Are you torn up to see that fool's wimpmobile get redecorated?

—You want the honest answer, I said, or the answer given by a responsible member of our society who respects the law?

—That's what I thought, he says, with a quick, slight smile.

We stand there for a second, watching a soccer game develop off at the far end of the playground. Without looking at me, Ernie speaks.

—So, Dooberman. What's it going to be? You going to bust us?

I watch a kid dribble through six or seven defenders, launch a shot that hits the crossbar, steal his rebound from the sweeper, and hit the crossbar again.

—I got nothing to bust anybody with, I say. I had a talk with a loyal teammate expressing support at a time when I was sulky and angry and needed it. I'm over that, the talk is over too, and we move on.

—That's the way to move all right, Ernie says. I can hear relief in his voice.

—I went to see Nathan last night.

—Yeah? he says. She quitting?

—No.

He nods. Good. Might as well hang in. Just got to stick to hockey, man, and get the people with agendas off our backs.

—Hockey's all that's happening, I say. We're three and oh, and we have to keep the good things going.

—Yeah, Ernie says, things like Kenny Moze.

We laugh, then wander back, and drift away from each other into groups of friends who are calling us.

Mack, the Mad Miata Mutilator. Live in peace, mate.

eight

I called Zip to ask if he wanted to do some skateboarding. It was something we had always done together, about the only thing he did not do with Kenny Moseby. They had always been best friends except for a while last fall when Zip was mad about K leaving the Wings for a year. I never mind doing something with *both* of them, but Kenny is so quiet and I am so talkative that sometimes I cannot help feeling that I'm being a hog or something, though I am not; you know how it is when you look at yourself as if you were someone else watching, and you think something about yourself that is untrue but still *looks* a certain way? The awareness can make you start acting un-natural, and when I become aware that I might look like I'm hogging Zip's attention I tend to shut up and Zip ends up with nobody to talk to and he gets cranky.

But Kenny does not skateboard; he will not risk

twisting an ankle or something that would keep him off the ice, and also I think he just has no interest in it. Zip, however, is awesome at skating and loves to do it whenever he isn't practicing goal-tending or hanging with Kenny. Last summer we even built a bunch of ollie platforms and grind rails and stuff to skate on. We store them in his garage.

—Skate? Sure, he said when I called. Come on over.

In ten minutes I was one-footing up his street and I saw he had already set up our junk in his driveway and was sitting on the curb guzzling a Jolt with another can beside him for me. I was still half a block away when he lowered the can to speak.

—You need new bearings. Those cruddy ones I warned you not to get are worn out already. You sound like a garbage truck going up a steep hill.

—And a good afternoon to you, too, I said. He was right about the bearings, though—they were going, and he *had* warned me not to buy them but to spend almost twice as much for the best kind, but I cheaped out so I'd have money left over for a movie or something. Zip always recommends getting the best mechanical stuff, even if it means waiting on a movie or a new CD or whatever. His motto is, Why not make use of the smarts of the guys who are trying to help us by discovering this material or design is more durable or smoother than the old one?

He tossed me the cola and I drank it in three swallows, and then we started to skate. In a few minutes it was obvious that although our little constructions still held some challenges for *me*, they didn't exactly push Zip into new territory. He didn't care or act bored or anything, but after a while I suggested stashing this junk real fast and heading down to the half-round pipe that was always left all over the place by the builders who kept adding to our development. On my way I had noticed where the latest projects were, and knew the crews were gone by now and we had just enough daylight left to get in some skating.

That's what we did. It turned out there were some great pipes left out on this particular day, a lot of really large half-rounds that got Zip going hard. He was cutting loose with his shuvits and kick flips and 360s and tail grinds and 50-50 grinds, while I was trying my little elementary moves, so that after a short time I was just as happy to sit back and watch him instead of skating more myself. Goalies don't get the chance on the ice to look graceful very much—once in a while they make a save that shows that beneath all that padding there is an athletic body, but more often they seem to be sprawling or lunging, as if their body were there for no purpose but to hurl the pads around in the way of shots.

But of course Zip could not be a great goalie if he weren't a great athlete, and great athletes are usually graceful in many kinds of movement besides their specialty. Zip makes his skateboard seem like a part of his own body that he easily commands by telepathy; it never looks like it is out of his control, or would just as soon go careening away guided by gravity or spin that was too crudely applied or just the perverse nature of wheels, the way mine does. It's like the board exists for one reason, and that reason is to give Zip speed and the freedom to almost fly. He concentrates so hard he doesn't look like he is having much fun, but a lot of hockey players are like that, me included—we're used to putting so much effort into something, we haven't got any ease left over for smiling and laughing or whatever the usual signs of fun are. In fact, we often look grim and tired and even bummed. But why would we do it if it weren't fun? Same with Zip on his board—he doesn't yell and grin, but he's enjoying himself.

After a while he came off a 360 and just skated the sides of the pipe to lose speed, and then skated over to where I was, hopped off his board, and took a seat.

—Who do you think did it? I asked, after he had panted for a few minutes.

He looked over at me. I assumed it was you, he said.

I tried not to get mad, since he was about the third person to make this assumption. Instead I said, Have you ever heard me call anyone 'pig'?

He thought it over. No, he said. That's true—it's not exactly your vocabulary.

—Next question. Who do you think was being called 'pig'?

He thought some more. Well, he said, I know where you're heading but I'll play along anyway. The facts make it easy: Nathan is *not* a pig, and her father *is*, so I'd have to say the word—after all, it was scratched on *his* car—was meant for him.

I nodded. Nathan doesn't agree, I said, and I think we ought to make sure she does.

He looked at me again. When did you develop this delicacy of feeling toward our fair captain? Last I saw, it was pretty clear you wished she would break both legs.

I winced. He started to apologize but I held up a hand. No, I said, it's me who should apologize, for *being* such a redass, and then for letting it show so much.

—Doober, when you go three hockey games without saying more than ten words, let's just say it's about what three hours of unchecked shrieking would be for anybody else. Which I mention so you'll see that it's more what you *didn't* do than what you *did*, so the unpleasantness was—well, actually, it was kind of a relief—

—Bite my nose.

—No, really, the fact is, we missed your big mouth. I mean it. I never knew before how much you keep the D in line, and other stuff too. I mean, within all that yabber-yabber there are pieces of wisdom, Doobs, which comes of course as a complete surprise.

—Well, I said, I guess I realized Nathan's okay and deserves to be treated that way.

—And her father's a bozo and deserves to be treated *that* way, so what's the problem?

—She told Coach she was quitting. Then she decided not to.

He shrugged. She's not that good, so it wouldn't hurt the team much, but it would be a shame to have her feeling so bad for no reason. I mean, we all resented her being shoved on us, but other than you we all decided to be gentlemen about it and I'd hate to see all our efforts at polite acceptance go to waste. I don't think anybody's made her feel bad until this car thing.

—Nobody but me, I said.

—Well, of course.

I must have looked pretty miserable because Zip slapped my back and said, Hey, come on, if I'd been told I was going to get captain and thereby gain the right to open my mouth even *more*, and some female took it away for no good reason, I too would have made her feel like doo-doo as much as possible.

—You would have?

—Of course.

—Then I guess it's lucky for her she got the C in *my* year and not *yours*.

—Absolutely, he said. I am not half as nice as you, *and* I would have been much *louder* and also I'm on the ice all the time and would thus miss no opportunity to undermine her confidence, which is shaky enough as it is.

We skated back to his house together, and then I took off for home. I must have had my head down in profound thought, because halfway there I ran somebody off the sidewalk and the person caught up with me and gave me a shove and I took a pretty good spill, but onto the grass, not the street.

—Hey! I said.

—Hey yourself, Hotwheels.

I recognized the voice. It was Nathan. She was carrying a pair of white-boot figure skates over her shoulder by the tied laces. They glowed in the twilight like things made of that special plastic that absorbs light.

—Sorry, I said. Then, realizing where we were,

I added, What are you doing over in *this* neighborhood?

—My mother lives over here, she said, seeming slightly nervous. See, last night I was with my dad, but tonight—

—Got it, I said. Don't worry; you're not the only person I know whose parents have split up and then designed complicated travel plans for the kids. You're more like the fiftieth.

—Okay, she said, sounding relieved. So you know.

—Yeah. But what's with the skates? Are you a hockey player with your dad, and a figure skater with your mom? Like, two lives or something?

—No, she said, looking at the skate in front. I— well, a long time ago I was, like, supposed to become a figure skater, but I wasn't talented enough to keep going with it until I won the gold medal at the Olympics, so it got dropped. But I still like to do the jumps once in a while, so I sneak out and go to a public skate and look like one of those showoffs who do such things. But I'm not much good, really.

—Why 'sneak'? And please don't tell me you change into one of those little skirt things.

—Not since I was eight. As for the sneaking—
well, let's just say my father took it hard that I
was not destined for skating glory, and it was a has-
sle to get him behind my decision to try playing
hockey, but once he switched he did it in a typically
overblown way, and would definitely regard it as
some kind of backsliding or reduction of my 'com-
mitment' if he caught me in these. Especially now,
after I had to talk him into letting me stay on the
team.

—What!?

She nodded. Yeah. After you left last night, after
you convinced me *not* to quit, he finally came in
and started talking as if of course I *was* going to
quit.

—Wait a minute. Did he hear you when you
told Coach you were quitting?

She shook her head.

—So you mean he came in and it was like *his*
idea?

—Right. He just *assumed* I would not associate
anymore with people who would treat me in such
a fashion.

—He assumed the car thing and the burning

pucks were aimed just at you? Nothing about himself?

—If you knew my father you wouldn't have to ask that. No, obviously the team was expressing its rejection of me—

—That's such a crock!

—I know, she said. I mean, I *guess* I know. Nobody's ever said or done anything rude before. Why wait until now?

—Because your father never put on *his* show before yesterday. But he wouldn't consider that.

—Never.

—He's a jerk.

—Congratulations on your insight.

—Did he even try to make you feel better and, like, urge you to stand up for yourself and face us vandals down?

—No. Far from it. He insisted I quit. As I said, I had to talk him into the idea that I was staying.

—*Why* did he want you to quit? What were his reasons?

—Probably afraid he'll get his next car trashed too. But he *said* it was because it was obvious this area was not ready to take an enlightened approach to female intrusion into male domains.

—Did you point out that yesterday was not your first day on a Wolfbay team, not even your first day as captain of the Peewees, and therefore the vandalism was obviously not the hotheaded, knee-jerk act of a threatened male? I mean, what does he think took us so long?

She shrugged. I realized too late that she was sick of the whole thing, and had probably been relieved to get to her mom's, take out the figure skates, get away from it until tomorrow's hockey practice at least. . . .

—Sorry, I said. I'm being a jerk to keep talking about it.

—It's okay. She sighed. People are often a lot worse than you're being. About him, I mean. They talk as if I had other options for a father. But, you know, it's like, Hey, he's what I got, and he's the *only* dad I've got, so . . .

—And of course the divorce is your fault too.

She looked shocked, but then she laughed. Yes, sometimes I take that on, too.

—How about the ozone layer? Is that one of your nasty little pieces of work, as well?

—Yes. She laughed. *And* the use of BHT in breakfast cereal.

—I thought as much. And we needn't even bother discussing responsibility for the increase of people's use of 'good' when they ought to say 'well' *or* the fact that Pakistan now has some plutonium and nuke capability.

—Mine. She laughed again. All mine. I'm just *awful*, am I not?

—You are indeed. Will you be the captain of my hockey team?

She stopped laughing and stared at me. What? she said.

—You heard me. I issued an invitation. What do you say?

She was still staring. Then in a very quiet voice she said, Yes. Yes, I'll do that.

—For me?

—No, she said.

—It has to be for me, at least first of all among your reasons from this point on, I said. It can be for your own self-actualization or for Zip or Coach Cooper next. But I'm asking you to do it, for me.

She watched me. You're not kidding, are you? she said.

I shook my head.

—Okay, she said. For you, then, first. Because I haven't been your captain yet, have I?

—I'm far too much of a gentleman to answer that, I said. See you at practice tomorrow. I skated off. Then I stopped, and turned, and said, Oh, and thank you for accepting my invitation.

—My pleasure, she said. Thanks for asking.

—No prob. 'Bye, Nathan.

—Good-bye, Doobs, she said.

nine

s we dress for the Hershey game, I sniff loudly and holler, What's that *smell*?

Everybody does like a one-take, some of them shooting me a quick look, because even though this is my usual routine whenever we play these guys, I guess my voice suddenly sounds *un*usual. Not for long, though.

—I said, *What's*—

—*Vanilla*! they finally holler back.

We do it twice more, louder each time, until we all start laughing and howling, with Prince's voice rising above the others as he indignantly insists it's *French* vanilla and there's even more howling.

I am sitting near Pincher, who has yet to get his first joke of the year.

—But I thought Hershey was the town where they made all that—

—Yes, Pinch, says Beckstein, you're right, but I

think the idea is, they've already *heard* every chocolate joke imaginable, is that right, Dooby? And besides, who wants to be called a vanilla hockey team?

—I think vanilla ice cream is *good,* Pinch whines.

—Fine, but we're talking about flavors associated with *hockey,* okay, Pinch? Sandy sighs and rolls his eyes at me.

—It's okay, Pinch, I say. You tell them all the chocolate jokes you want.

—Yeah, says Cody. What'll happen is, you'll start one, and they'll finish it and tell you another, and another, and another. . . .

—So chocolate jokes have become something they've turned into *their* thing, see, Pinch?

—I get it, he says with a pout, looking into his bag.

—If you're looking for your wit, says Prince, here it is. He holds one of Pinch's gloves out to him. Pinch looks at it, looks at Prince to see if he is maybe being mocked some more, but Prince gives it a shake and says, Come on.

—Thanks. I was wondering where it got to, says Pinch loudly, taking the glove and putting it on. He waits, but nobody says anything mocking, so he breathes out a big one. Then he looks at me. Guy can't play on a team with Dooby too long if he's lost his wit, he says.

—He can play a whole season *this* far at least, says Woodsie.

I look over at him a little mad. He gives me the look right back.

—Well, I say, still holding Woodsie's eyes, I've just been giving somebody else—*anybody*—the chance to step up and show some leadership in the area of wise and witty communication. But all of you bozos have been so quiet I concluded it was up to me after all.

—Except for Kenny, that is, says Prince, shaking his head. We cannot get *that* dude to shut *up*.

—A player has to go with his *natural* strength, Prince, says Cody. Kenny's natural strength is scoring five or six goals a game and making three or four amazing defensive saves. So we have to learn to place value on his contribution, and can't expect him to be the Mouth *too*. But Dooby—well, he *has* no other hockey strengths besides yapping, so let's look to him for *that*, little though it may be in terms of a contribution.

—No, says Zip. You're forgetting something. Doobs is *awesome* at making crisp line changes.

Everyone laughs. Coach Cooper yells at us all the time to make our line changes *crisp*, instead of, as he puts it, straggly.

Just then the door opens and Coach steps in.

—What do *you* want? I yell at him. Don't you know there's an unwritten no-parents clause in the code of the locker room? Do you realize how much you stand to humiliate Cody?

Cody has hidden his face in his sweater.

—Oh. Sorry, says the coach, and, just like that, he leaves. But he sticks his head back in just long enough to say, Nice to have you back, Doober.

—*Out!* I scream.

He does not return, even to tell us to take the ice. Nathan has to go out and check the Zamboni's progress, and she decides when we hit the ice for warm-ups. Coach is already on the bench, making some notes on the index card he always holds through every game. We once asked Cody if he had ever gotten ahold of one of his father's cards and he said he had, and that they all said the same thing on them: THE WINNER IS THE TEAM WITH A

HIGHER NUMBER OF GOALS AT THE END OF THE GAME.

—What about ties? Pincher said.

—Please, said Cody. That's an advanced concept we'll be ready to introduce only after this more elementary one has been mastered.

Anyway, we do warm-ups, I guess, and like old times I don't really notice because I am chattering again, telling Prince his left boot lace is not double-knotted like his right so he'd better see to it, telling Ernie the idea is to shoot *after* he has controlled the puck on his stickblade, not *before*, suggesting to Sandy that he begin a Victory Beard like the NHL guys do in the playoffs when they get all scruffy and fuzzy until they lose, chatter chatter chatter.

And then the horn blows and we go to the bench and then I'm back out on the ice and the game starts.

—Your mouthguard is leaking, I tell the left wing. Better fix it, that's a two-minute minor in Maryland.

—What does a leaking mouthguard—

By then I have knocked his stick a foot off the ice and a pass to him comes to me instead and I fake to the inside but go past him up the boards and cross the blue line at full speed with the puck, screaming, We cheated! We cheated! I am really a center and we have only one defenseman on the ice! and then I drop a pass backhand between my skates because I have *always* wanted to do that and Cody picks it up and flips it in over the goalie's shoulder.

I skate by the bench. That's my first assist, I say, and I want the puck. In fact, I want *all* the pucks.

—Same line, says the coach. No change.

—Good idea, I tell him, then I ask the left wing if he thinks it's a good idea.

—What—he starts to say as Prince wins the face-off and Barry fires it into the far corner and the wing is the last guy to get into the zone, and his man, who is me, gets the puck on a pass back from Prince in the corner and because there is no one covering me I skate it all the way to the top of the circle, then cut straight across and for a second draw two men to check me and at just that moment backhand another pass, this one a sharp diagonal against the flow of the play, to Boot at the far post, and he buries it.

—Change, says the Coach, above the roar and

the whacking of sticks against the bench boards.

—I'm not changing, I tell him, until I feel I can do it crisply.

—Get off the ice, you loony. He laughs. I sit down.

Nathan is about to take the face-off.

—Nathan! I holler. She looks up.

—*You* take the face-off, I tell her.

She shakes her head and bends down again. She wins the face-off and Kenny gets it. He does not score during this shift but he does get four shots on goal. Nathan knocks in one of the rebounds. To everyone's surprise she fishes the puck out of the net and picks it up, says something brief to the ref and he nods, and she detours on her way to the center-ice face-off to skate by the bench and flip me the puck.

—Bite on this, she says, and you'll feel better.

—Did she tell you that was her first goal or something? I holler at the ref. Don't believe her! She does this with all the boys!

After the first it's up to 5–0 and the Hershey team decides to save its energy for its afternoon game against Reston. The players just go through the motions, despite my yelled protests that they are a bunch of chickenhearts playing vanilla hockey. We win 9–0 only because Coach sits Kenny for the whole third period to rest a slightly pulled hamstring.

During the handshakes, the Hershey coach tells me, That's quite a mouth you got on you.

—I borrowed it from a friend and I'll be sure to tell him you liked it. And by the way, you guys *are* chickenhearted for giving up so early. And your team isn't good enough to act like they can just turn it off and on when you want them to.

—We'll be sure to turn it on all the way when we get you up to Hershey, he says.

—Better worry about turning it on in Reston first, I say.

(I find out later that Reston beats them 6–2 in the afternoon.)

In the locker room afterward Zip and I do our routine where we pretend to be basketball players escaped from an insane asylum who think we just played a game of hoops, and Prince sings three songs, and in the moment of silence after the applause Sandy Beckstein says, Can we ever turn him off?

—With that voice, who would want to turn Prince off? I say.

—I wasn't talking about—oh. Got me.

Because everybody's laughing at him.

Here's a sneak peek at the next book in the

Wolfbay Wings ice hockey

series by Bruce Brooks

available from HarperCollins

aybe that's why I didn't make the A's—I didn't do the best I could. After the fifth goal I had two more great shots, but I passed to a linemate instead, not wanting to hog the scoring, see. By the way, both of these passes got immediately buried in rope, so I had two assists to offset the five G's, a sign of some playmaking skills too, you know.

But I was cut. Snipped. Eliminated. Dropped. The bozoid coach, a yuppie with wire-rim glasses and a Fila warm-up suit worn above the CCM 952 skates ($400 a pair, Jack) that he put to *good* use cruising along the red line at 2 mph while he watched us play 90 feet away, had the incredible stupid nerve to tell me, when I had seen the cut list and rode my bike over to his *house*, "If you'd scored four goals, you might have made the team. If you'd scored three, almost certainly. Two goals, definitely you're on the roster. One goal and you might even be centering the first line."

It was his cute little way of telling me he thought I was too selfish, too *offensively motivated*, for the team, see. Subtle, isn't he?

I said to this guy, "Last time I checked, the team with the most goals was the winner. Maybe I heard wrong. Maybe now they award the victory to, like, the team that makes the prettiest soft-hands passes in the neutral zone."

He said, "There's more to hockey than speed and flashy moves and a great shot, Reed."

"Right: There's also goaltending, but usually goalies handle that part."

He shook his head with another weary smile.

When I got home both of my brothers were in the kitchen, drinking some of my dad's Schlitz and waiting. "So?" said Bo.

"So what?"

Pete looked at Bo and burped and grinned and said, "I told you he'd blow it. He didn't make 'em."

Bo started to smile but tried to hold it until he heard it from me. "Did you? Make the A's?"

"Kiss off," I said, and he exploded into laughing. When he laughs he sprays his disgusting spittle all over the place. He and Pete slapped high fives and howled together.

Bo said, "What punishment do you think is appropriate, Pete?"

Pete acted like he was considering many wonderful options. "Well, at the very least we shave his head for starters."

I have hair down to the middle of my back. Took me almost two years to grow it right.

A kind of light bulb went on behind Bo's eyes. He nudged Pete and leaned close and said something I couldn't hear. Pete let out a single honk of laughter, and said, "Excellent." Then they both started walking toward me.

"Shampoo time," said Bo.

"Then a little trim," said Pete.